SEARCH FOR THE GOLDEN CITY

BY GREG FARSHTEY

SCHOLASTIC INC.

New York Toronto London Auckland Sydney
Mexico City New Delhi Hong Kong Buenos Aires

No part of this publication may be reproduced in whole or part, stored in a
retrieval system, or transmitted in any form or by any means, electronic, mechanical,
photocopying, recording, or otherwise, without written permission of the publisher.
For information regarding permission, write to Scholastic Inc.,
Attention: Permissions Department, 557 Broadway, New York, NY 10012.

ISBN-13: 978-0-439-89203-2
ISBN-10: 0-439-89203-1

12 11 10 9 8 7 6 5 4 3 2 1   7 8 9 10 11/0

Printed in the U.S.A.
First printing, March 2007

CHAPTER 1

Takeshi walked away and tried not to look back. He and his best friends, Hikaru and Ryo, were starting what could be a long and dangerous journey. They were leaving behind Sentai Fortress, which had been their home for more than a year. Takeshi knew their mission was a matter of life and death, but it was still hard to say good-bye.

As Takeshi worked the controls of his Grand Titan battle machine, he remembered the first time he had ever seen Sentai Fortress. It was years ago, after the first war between humans and robots. Takeshi worked as a miner and lived with his parents and baby sister. When the robots rebelled a second time, striking hard and fast and taking over the entire southern half of Sentai Mountain, his family had gone missing in all the confusion.

Desperate to find his loved ones again, he went to Sentai Fortress to meet with the wise leader of the human village, Sensei Keiken. The Sensei invited him to join a new team being formed to fight the robots. It was called EXO-FORCE. Takeshi said yes and spent months training to learn how to operate a battle machine.

Takeshi and the EXO-FORCE team would fight in many great battles against the robots. The most recent was by far the most challenging. Takeshi was the hero of that fight, defeating the robots' Striking Venom battle machine and saving the day. But Sentai Fortress had been badly damaged. Everyone in the EXO-FORCE team knew the robots would attack again sometime soon. Maybe next time the fortress would not survive.

"We have to find new technology we can use to defeat the robots," Sensei Keiken had said. "I have heard legends of a great Golden City somewhere high up the mountain. According to the tales, incredible discoveries were made there. We must find this city! It is the only way to win this fight and save humanity."

Takeshi, Hikaru, and Ryo volunteered to go and search for the Golden City. They did not know how long the search would take, or even if the Golden City actually existed. But they knew they had to try and find it, no matter how hard it was to leave friends and family behind.

Neither Takeshi, Hikaru, nor Ryo had ever traveled too far up the mountain, although Hikaru had gotten a good view of it from the air. The peak of the mountain looked very beautiful. There were plenty of trees and streams—very different from what they were used to. The area around

Sentai Fortress had been scarred by all the battles fought there.

The trip up the mountain was hard. There was no clear path, just steep climbs and dense woods. Although Hikaru's battle machine, the Silent Strike, could fly, the Sensei had ordered that he stay on the ground as much as possible on the journey. The Sensei didn't want the robots to spot them searching for the Golden City.

"I just realized something," said Hikaru, as he fought the controls to get the Silent

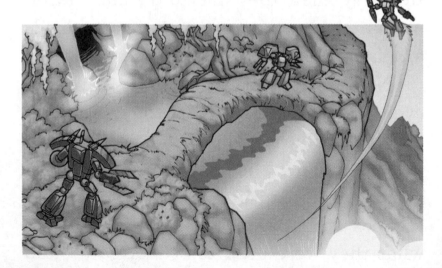

Strike through a narrow gap between two boulders.

"What?" asked Takeshi.

"Huge, armored battle machines really weren't made for hiking," Hikaru answered.

光　　光　　光

"Are we there yet?" Ryo asked. They had been journeying for several hours now, with no sign of the Golden City.

Hikaru checked the scanners on his battle machine's control panel. "I'm not seeing anything on my sensors—no city, no robots, nothing."

Takeshi made the Grand Titan's arm point toward a clearing. "It's getting dark. We should make camp there. I'll take the first watch."

The three pilots climbed out of their battle machines and set up camp. After a quick meal, Takeshi got back into the Grand Titan and piloted it to the edge of the clearing. Hikaru and Ryo unrolled their sleeping bags and tried to get some sleep. After a few minutes, Ryo asked, "How much do we really know about this Golden City?"

"According to the Sensei, the Golden City existed long before any human settlements were built on Sentai Mountain," said Hikaru. "No one knows for sure who built it or how it's stayed hidden for so long. Legend says the city contains secret wisdom and amazing technology."

"Do you think it really exists?" Ryo asked. "Or is it just a story?"

"I don't know," said Hikaru. "The Sensei says it's real and he's usually right about things. So get some sleep and maybe we will find it tomorrow."

Takeshi was in his battle machine, wondering about the same thing . . . were they on a wild goose chase? Right now, though, he had something else to worry about. While his sensor scans showed the area around the clearing free of any robots or robot battle machines, his audio receivers were picking up noises from nearby. They sounded like metal scraping against metal.

He checked his weapons. They were powered up and ready. Ryo, a genius mechanic, had done fast work repairing the Grand Titan after the last battle. Takeshi hoped that it wouldn't break down at a crucial moment.

Another sound came from his left.

Takeshi turned the battle machine to face that direction. The next thing he knew, a laser blast had hit the Grand Titan from behind, sending his battle machine flying toward the trees where Hikaru and Ryo were camped.

The Grand Titan hit hard, splintering centuries-old trees. Takeshi glanced at his sensor screen, which still showed no enemies in the area. *Something's really wrong here,* he thought to himself. *And if I don't figure it out soon, I might not live to figure it out at all.*

Takeshi hit the controls and made the Grand Titan rise to its feet. This time he could see his attackers. Two robot battle machines had emerged from the woods, but they were nothing like he had seen before. They were green and black, three-legged mechanical vehicles that reminded him of insects. Each was piloted by a Devastator robot. But what really struck Takeshi was

the clear pod mounted on top, containing a human prisoner.

One machine was blasting in the Grand Titan's direction, while the other was firing at Hikaru and Ryo, trying to prevent them from reaching their battle machines. Takeshi aimed and fired his battle machine's laser cannon at the side of the mountain. Just as he planned, a great slab of rock knocked into the robot machine, throwing it off balance. Hikaru and Ryo took advantage of the opportunity to climb into their battle machines and power up.

"Friends of yours?" Hikaru broadcast to Takeshi. "And how come my sensors still show nothing there?"

"Those two buckets-of-bolts battle machines are new to me," Takeshi replied. "Forget the sensors. Just point and shoot!"

The robots weren't going to stand around and be targets. Seeing that their first attack had failed, both robot battle machines disappeared back into the woods. Hikaru piloted the Silent Strike straight up into the air, but couldn't see them or pick them up on his scanners. He was ready to go search for them, but Takeshi signaled him to come back down.

"Ryo says it's a cloaking device," Takeshi said.

"Just like what was in your old Stealth Hunter armor," Ryo explained. "You won't know they're coming until they're here."

"What about those human prisoners we saw in the pods?" asked Hikaru.

Takeshi frowned. "The robots are getting smarter. If they have a human inside their battle machines, they know we won't attack at full power. We wouldn't risk harming the human prisoners. The robots see mercy and loyalty as weaknesses. They are going to use them against us."

Ryo and Hikaru looked around at the jutting peaks and the ancient trees. Suddenly, the night seemed very dark and the wind very cold.

CHAPTER 2

After a sleepless night, Hikaru, Takeshi, and Ryo were back in their battle machines and on the move again before dawn. Their control panels showed that all their weapons were powered up and their battle machines were operating perfectly. But they could not escape the feeling that they were being watched.

As they climbed higher, the path became steeper and more dangerous. Hikaru flew ahead to scout, but Takeshi and Ryo were left to struggle on land up the peaks.

"Why can't we just blast out a tunnel with our weapons?" Ryo asked.

"Too dangerous," Takeshi replied. "The mountain was split in half during the first war between humans and robots, there's no telling what other damage was done. Start firing lasers and you could cause a —"

Takeshi's answer was drowned out by a rumbling sound coming from higher up the mountain. "Rock slide!" Hikaru shouted.

Huge boulders were rolling down the mountainside, right for Takeshi and Ryo in their battle machines. "Blast them!" Takeshi shouted into his battle machine's radio.

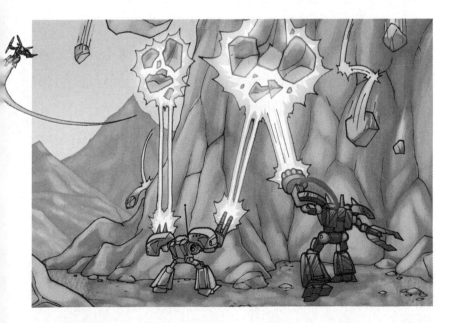

All three pilots triggered their weapons at once. The combined power of the Grand Titan, Uplink, and Silent Strike battle machines shattered the boulders into pebbles.

"Anyone think that rock slide was an accident?" Takeshi asked.

"I did at first," said Ryo, pointing up at the sky. "But I just changed my mind."

Two robot battle machines dove out of the sky toward the EXO-FORCE members. They were yellow and black, both with wings and a nasty-looking rocket launcher mounted on the right arm. Hikaru shot across the sky in the Silent Strike, firing as he went, but narrowly missing the rapidly moving robot machines. Takeshi and Ryo used the time to find cover.

The Devastator pilot in the nearest machine glanced toward the oncoming Silent Strike. "Iron Condor-2 recording," he said in a cold, mechanical voice. "EXO-

FORCE battle machine code-named Silent Strike identified. Activating attack option Y44."

The Iron Condor fired its launcher at the Silent Strike. Hikaru tried to dodge the attack, but the rocket followed him wherever he flew. There was no escape! When the rocket struck the Silent Strike, it unleashed a wave of magnetic energy. The arms of the Silent Strike suddenly clamped down against the body of the battle machine while the legs slammed together. The Silent Strike had become a giant magnet! Now none of the machine's limbs could be moved. The battle machine could still fly, but aiming or firing weapons was now impossible.

Cute trick, buckethead, Hikaru thought. *I can't aim my weapons or do any complicated maneuvers. I always knew I might not come back from one of these battles—but I'm not ready to lose today!*

Hikaru expected the robots to take

advantage of the situation and finish him off, but to his surprise the Iron Condors flew wide and went after the Grand Titan and Uplink. Then, instead of firing their launchers at the Grand Titan and Uplink, the Iron Condors flew close to the ground and began grappling with their enemies.

I'm an easy target and they ignore me, thought Hikaru. *Instead, they go wrestle with the Grand Titan. How come? Unless . . . unless . . .*

"Takeshi!" Hikaru shouted. "Throw one this way!"

Down below, Takeshi nodded. The Iron Condor was a powerful battle machine, but not as strong or well armored as the Grand Titan. With a great effort, he broke the Iron Condor's grip and hurled the robot battle machine toward the Silent Strike.

As it came nearer, the Iron Condor picked up speed. It was being drawn by the magnetic pull of the Silent Strike, and the robot pilot could not break away.

Hikaru smiled. *I thought so,* he said to himself. *They turned the Silent Strike into a magnet—and a magnet would attract their battle machines! That's why they had to stay far away.*

Then his smile faded. *It's going to smash right into me!*

Helpless in the grip of magnetism, the Iron Condor smashed into the Silent Strike. Sparks flew in both cockpits. The robot pilot tried to push the EXO-FORCE battle machine away, but now the arms and legs of his machine weren't working either. The two battle machines were stuck together!

Hikaru put every bit of his power into his thrusters and flew straight for a jagged peak. At the last moment, the robot pilot realized what he was going to do and ejected to safety. The next second, Hikaru maneuvered the two fused battle machines so that the Iron

Condor struck the peak. The sharp rock slammed into the robot battle machine and scraped it right off of the Silent Strike. The fragments of the Iron Condor tumbled down the side of the mountain.

The other Iron Condor was having better luck with Uplink. Before the Grand Titan could stop it, the Iron Condor had grabbed Uplink and flown up into the sky with it. Ryo fought the controls to try to break Uplink free of the Iron Condor's grip. The Grand Titan fired from below, trying to bring the Iron Condor down, but missed.

The arms and legs of the Silent Strike suddenly snapped free. The magnetic effect of the robot rocket had faded! Hikaru piloted the Silent Strike in hot pursuit of the Iron Condor. But the robot machine had too big a lead, and it seemed certain it would get away with its prisoner.

"We have to stop it!" Hikaru yelled.

"I'm trying!" said Takeshi, firing another

blast toward the fleeing Iron Condor. "But it's already out of range!"

"Wait a second," Hikaru said. "It's diving ..."

He checked his sensors. They matched what his eyes were telling him. The Iron Condor had suddenly swooped low to the ground and let go of Uplink. The EXO-FORCE battle machine hit the ground, but not hard enough to do any real damage. Then the Iron Condor flew off, leaving very confused EXO-FORCE pilots behind.

Hikaru flew the Silent Strike over to retrieve Ryo and Uplink. "How did you escape?" he asked.

"If you find out, tell me," Ryo replied. "I tried everything I could and that rustbucket wouldn't let go of Uplink. Then it suddenly drops me off like it was just giving me a ride home."

"Strange," said Hikaru. "It must have gotten new orders. Come on, I will fly you back to Takeshi and we can get moving again."

The Silent Strike grabbed on to Uplink and flew back toward the battle site. Neither Hikaru nor Ryo noticed an almost microscopic piece of equipment now attached magnetically to Uplink's right shoulder plate. It had been a "gift" from the Iron Condor before the robot battle machine gave up the fight. Its job was to help bring about the end of the EXO-FORCE team, and it had already begun to work.

光　　光　　光

On the other side of the mountain lay an ugly building made of scorched and blackened metal. It was surrounded by dozens of Sentry battle machines piloted by Iron Drone robots. Weapons were mounted on the roof of the building and on the grounds surrounding the building. This was the headquarters of the robot rebellion. Here, plans were made and battle machines built, all with only one goal: the conquest of humanity and ultimate power for robots.

Inside, Meca One, the golden robot leader, was watching a giant viewscreen. The image on the viewscreen showed the Grand Titan and the Silent Strike as they resumed their journey up Sentai Mountain. Based on the camera angle, Uplink had to have been behind them but was not visible on the screen. The human pilots were talking about their mission, and Meca One

could now hear every word.

The robot leader was satisfied that all was proceeding as planned. The electronic bugging device planted by the Iron Condor on the Uplink battle machine was operating perfectly, relaying everything the EXO-FORCE members said or saw back to the robot base. As long as none of the humans suspected they were being monitored, the robots would learn everything they did on their journey.

Shortly after the first attack by the Shadow Crawler battle machines, the robot pilots had informed headquarters that the humans were definitely heading up the mountain. Meca One had tried to compute their probable course, but could come up with no reason why three EXO-FORCE pilots would be making such a journey. There was only one way to find out what the robots needed to know: plant a monitoring device on one of the human battle machines.

Meca One sat down to watch and listen. The robot leader was sure this would be a most valuable program.

CHAPTER 3

"So the Golden City has new technology—and maybe new weapons?" Ryo said. "That still doesn't explain who built it, or why they haven't come to help us fight the robots."

"Maybe the city's inhabitants are all long dead," Hikaru replied. "Or maybe they just think we should solve our own problems."

"Or maybe the Golden City is just what it sounds like: a legend," Ryo snapped. "What if we get to the top of the mountain and there's nothing there?"

"Then consider this a nature hike," said Hikaru, smiling. "You could use the exercise, Ryo."

光　光　光

Back at Sentai Fortress, EXO-FORCE headquarters, Sensei Keiken was pacing the floor. He knew that Takeshi, Hikaru, and Ryo had not been gone long enough to have found the city, but he was still anxious for word. What if something had happened? What if they had been attacked by the robots and needed help? Or had found the Golden City and run into some kind of automatic defenses?

Getting the answers would mean taking a huge risk. If he sent out a radio transmission, the robots might trace it to the EXO-FORCE squad. The whole mission, and the lives of Hikaru, Takeshi, and Ryo, would be endangered.

He looked at the image of Meca One he kept always on one screen. It was good to keep the face of the enemy in mind. *What is going through your computerized brain right now, you metal monster?* the Sensei wondered. *How long before your robots attack again as part of your mad quest to conquer humanity?*

The Sensei made a decision. He had to know his three pilots were okay and what they might have discovered.

"Send a priority signal to the Grand Titan," Keiken ordered his communications officer. "Coded and scrambled. Tell Takeshi I want a status report."

Keiken looked back to the image of Meca One. *Plot and plan all you like, robot,* he thought. *Before this is all done, I'll see you taken apart, bolt by bolt, and turned into scrap.*

"Message sent, Sensei," reported the communications officer. "Waiting for reply."

光　　光　　光

"Message being broadcast from Sentai Fortress to EXO-FORCE squad," stated a Devastator robot. "Instructions, Meca One?"

"What does the message say?"

"Insufficient data to respond," said the Devastator. "Message is scrambled for security."

"Jam the signal!" ordered Meca One. "The EXO-FORCE pilots will have to travel in silence. What the Sensei doesn't know, won't help him."

光　光　光

For Hikaru, Takeshi, and Ryo, there was good news and there was bad news. The good news was that they were almost at the very top of the mountain, meaning their journey had to end soon. The bad news was that they hadn't seen anything that looked like a Golden City.

"Something's wrong," said Takeshi. "Something's really wrong."

"What is it?" asked Hikaru. "Your battle machine breaking down?"

"Hey!" snapped Ryo. "I did a great job repairing the Grand

Titan, especially considering the inside of it was all melted metal and fused wires. So if something's gone wrong with it—"

"Nothing has—at least, I don't think so," said Takeshi. "This mass scanner on the control panel shows the size of any objects up ahead. I was scanning farther up the mountain and it's reading something huge. But nothing is showing up on any other scanner."

"Maybe another robot battle machine invisible to sensors?" suggested Hikaru.

"No, they wouldn't show up on that scanner," Ryo answered. "I tested that panel myself, it's perfect. Something's up there, guys—something we can't see."

"So what do we do?" asked Takeshi. "Just keep walking until we bump into it?"

Ryo didn't answer. Instead, he scrambled around inside Uplink's cockpit until he found the special tools he was looking for. Then he opened the battle machine's control panel and started snipping wires and rearranging components.

"Done!" he yelled, a big smile on his face.

"With what?" asked Hikaru.

"I changed the sensors in Uplink so that they can pick up sources of energy," Ryo said. "If something is hidden up above, you can bet it takes a lot of energy to keep it that way. And once we find —ah-hah!"

Ryo fiddled with the scanner controls furiously, but didn't say anything about what he had seen. After a moment, Hikaru turned to Takeshi, saying, "I hate it when he does that."

"Two energy sources—one huge, one small," said Ryo. "Small one is out in front of the big one. That explains it!"

"You lost me back on 'ah-hah,'" said

Hikaru. "What explains what?"

"Don't you get it?" replied Ryo. "Okay, Takeshi's mass scanner says there's something big up there, but we can't see it. The mass scanner can't be wrong—I built it—which means there must be something there, but it's invisible."

"Right," said Hikaru.

"It takes power to conceal something that big," Ryo continued. "The smaller power source I just found has to be the generator for the invisibility field. Smash it, and we'll be able to see whatever it's hiding."

"About time we had something to smash," Takeshi said. "I was getting cranky."

Ryo led his partners up a rocky incline to a plateau. "The smaller source of power is right in front of us, even though we can't see it," he said. "Takeshi, want to take it out?"

Takeshi took aim with the Grand Titan's rotating laser cannon and fired where

Ryo said the target was located. Nothing happened.

"How can that be?" asked Takeshi. "Why isn't the ground shattering from the blast?"

"You're not hitting the ground," Ryo replied. "You're hitting the generator, just not hard enough."

Hikaru and Ryo tried blasting at the same spot with Silent Strike and Uplink, but it made no difference. "Only one thing left to try," said Hikaru. "We hit it all together. On three—one . . . two . . . three!"

All three battle machines fired at once. There was an explosion and a burst of bright light, followed by a powerful jolt of electricity. The energy struck the battle machines, causing sparks to leap from the control panels, circuits to fuse, and wires to melt. The pilots jumped out as smoke filled the cockpits.

Takeshi looked grimly at his ruined Grand Titan. The others did the same.

"Well, that went great. We ruined three battle machines, and for what?"

"For that," said Hikaru, pointing at a massive golden city shimmering in the distance. All three pilot stared in awe at what was appearing before their eyes.

CHAPTER 4

"It's . . . amazing," Ryo said quietly.

"It looks old and brand-new at the same time," said Hikaru. "How is that possible?"

Takeshi examined the wreckage of the generator on the ground in front of him. This had been the device that had kept the Golden City hidden from view behind an invisibility screen. It didn't look like much now, and probably hadn't when it was intact. But it had been powerful enough to conceal an entire city and fry three battle machines. *Could be its appearance isn't the only one that's deceiving around here,* he thought.

"First question we have to answer is whether or not anyone is living here,"

Takeshi said. "And if they are, I hope they're friendly, because our battle machines aren't much good right now."

Cautiously, he stepped through the gates of the city. Inside, each building looked as if it had been shaped from molten gold. If the place were to be melted down, it would be worth a fortune. Strangely, though, no one seemed to be living there. The only sounds were the EXO-FORCE pilots' footsteps

and the wind howling around the golden towers.

"Where did all the people go?" asked Hikaru.

"I don't know. It almost looks like no one ever lived here," Ryo answered. "None of the buildings or streets show any signs of age or wear. This is . . . spooky."

"We should radio back to base, but with our battle machines wrecked, that's out," said Takeshi. "We'll scout around and then head back to make a report. Wait until the Sensei hears we found it!"

光　　光　　光

Meca One needed a new plan. The humans had advanced on foot into the Golden City, leaving the damaged Uplink outside. That meant the Uplink's monitor was now useless. Meca One could not see what was going on inside the city or hear what the humans were saying.

The robot leader slapped a control switch on the communications panel. "Order a squad of Iron Condors into the air, and send a team of Shadow Crawlers over the high bridges," Meca One commanded. "The three EXO-FORCE pilots are out of their battle machines and unarmed. Seize them and the city."

A moment later, three Iron Condors soared from the base, heading for the Golden City. It was only a matter of time now.

If this new city was your last hope, Sensei, thought Meca One, *then that hope is about to be crushed.*

"What is that?" asked Hikaru. "It looks like something Ryo would build in his spare time."

The three pilots were standing in a massive chamber inside the biggest building in the city. The vaulted ceiling must have been at least 100 feet above the floor. The walls were golden with what looked like circuitry patterns engraved in the metal. In the center of the room was a machine bigger than anything any of them had ever seen. It looked like a computer, but one far more powerful than even the ones at Sentai Fortress.

"It's not making any noise. I think it's turned off," said Ryo.

"Let it stay that way," Takeshi ordered. "The Sensei will know what to do with it."

"Still, it won't hurt to take a look," Ryo answered, taking a step forward. The second he did so, the machine flared to life. Red, green, and blue lights began flashing on the control panels and a loud hum filled the air. Ryo took a quick step back, but nothing changed.

"Please enter code," the machine said in a voice that sounded almost human.

"What? What code?" said Ryo.

"Please enter code," it repeated.

"Over here!" Hikaru said. Affixed to the

wall was a narrow plate with a random assortment of numbers and letters on it. "At first, I thought it was part of the metal, but it's stuck on through magnetism. See?" He pulled it loose and handed it to Ryo.

"That sure looks like a code," said the engineer. "Should I enter it?"

"I don't think—" Takeshi began. He was cut off by the sound of the chamber doors slamming shut behind them. Rushing over, he discovered they were locked in.

"Please enter code," the machine said again.

"Well, if you insist," Ryo answered. He walked over to the keypad and punched in the numbers and letters. When he was done, the machine's hum softened and the voice spoke again.

"Code accepted," it said. "Welcome. You have been granted access to this machine's first level of data. To access other information, please enter the correct code."

"What other information?" Ryo asked. He turned to his friends, saying, "What does it mean?" Hikaru and Takeshi shook their heads, as much in the dark as Ryo.

"This unit contains all the data put into it by the builders of this city," the machine responded.

Ryo jumped. "You can answer? You can have conversations?" he said to the machine, surprised.

"This unit is programmed to understand and respond to all known languages—a simple operation requiring only the tiniest fraction of my processing power," the computer replied. "To be more specific, it requires .0000000000001 divided by—"

"Got it, okay," Ryo interrupted. "Now what other information were you talking about?"

"This unit contains math and science data, history, blueprints for weapons, armor and other technology, vehicle descriptions and building instructions, geological and climate data, chemical tables—"

"Stop!" said Ryo. "Weapons and armor—how do we find out about that?"

"You will need to enter the correct codes in the correct sequence. With each code, you will gain access to more information. You will also need basic equipment in order to use this data."

Three slots slid open in the walls of the chamber to reveal three battle

machines. Images of them also appeared on the computer's main screen. The red armor was identified as Blade Titan, the blue and white as Sky Guardian, and the green and white machine as Cyclone Defender.

"Wow!" said Hikaru, rushing over to the Sky Guardian. "Even you could learn something from these guys, Ryo!"

"Please enter code for more data," the computer said. "Code is located at coordinates X257 and Y136." A map flashed on the screen. It showed that those coordinates matched a building on the southern end of the city. A second later, the doors of the chamber unlocked and swung open.

"Let's go!" said Ryo, running outside. Suddenly, he turned around and ran back in. "Or not!"

Takeshi looked outside. Three Iron Condors were diving toward the building, and he could see two Shadow Crawlers coming through the city gates.

"I hope these battle machines work!" he yelled, racing for the Blade Titan. "Get in and see if you can figure out how to work these things!"

Takeshi climbed into the cockpit and looked at the instrument panel. All the controls were in a language he didn't recognize. He spotted a big red button in the upper right-hand corner of the panel and decided it looked like a "start" button. *At least I hope that's what it is,* he said to himself. *With my luck, it's probably a self-destruct button.*

He slammed his hand down on the button. The battle machine's instrument panel lit up. Takeshi grabbed what looked like a control rudder and eased it forward. The Blade Titan responded by charging forward like a tank, smashing part of the wall in the process.

"Oh, yes," Takeshi said, smiling. "I think this machine and I are going to get along just fine!"

CHAPTER 5

The Iron Condors took an attack stance and waited for the Shadow Crawlers to do the same. There was no need to hurry. After all, the EXO-FORCE machines were no longer a threat.

Suddenly, their sensors picked up something emerging from the building in front of them. By the time their high-speed computer minds processed the data, the object was already past them and circling to come back. This did not compute—there were no unauthorized robot battle machines in the vicinity, and no human-made machine could move that fast.

Two of the Iron Condors turned to meet

the attack. Both fired their launchers, but their target evaded them with ease. The robot battle machines veered off, each going in a different direction.

In the cockpit of the Sky Guardian, Hikaru was having the time of his life. He was sure he could fly rings around the robots in this machine. But this wasn't the time for stunts. He had to defeat the Iron Condors before they did any damage to the

Golden City. Hikaru hit the button he was sure would power up the battle machine's weapons.

There was no result. A glance at the power levels told the story: As long as the Sky Guardian was moving this fast, there was no energy left over for the weapons.

"Okay, then slow down," Hikaru said, pulling back on the rudder. But the battle machine had just picked up speed. "Come on, stop!" Now the Sky Guardian had flown past the city and was heading for a mountain peak. Nothing Hikaru could do would slow it down.

He was searching for some kind of an "off" switch when he noticed one button was flashing red. With nothing else to try, he hit it. The battle machine immediately slowed down as power levels for the weapons rose.

"Just what I need," Hikaru muttered, "a battle machine with cruise control."

On the ground, Takeshi was having better luck with his new machine. It was equipped with a multi-barreled proton cannon. Takeshi wasn't sure just what the weapon could do, but he was willing to bet it involved big explosions. Unfortunately, he was up against Shadow Crawlers, complete with prison pods on top containing human prisoners. Aim too high or fire too powerful a blast and he might injure or kill the humans.

The Shadow Crawlers had no such worry and were blasting away at the Blade Titan. The human battle machine's shields deflected the blasts, but it was going to take more than a good defense to win this battle.

Takeshi frowned. His first attempt to fire the proton cannon had resulted in the cannon shifting to point right at his own cockpit! After getting that undone, he hit half a dozen other buttons, resulting in everything from the radio's volume going up to the cockpit popping open. Now he thought he had finally found the firing button. Crossing his fingers, he hit the button.

It was worth the wait. The multiple proton bursts sheared off one of the front legs of the first Shadow Crawler, sending it toppling forward. Seeing that, the second Shadow Crawler backed off.

Whoever designed these machines and these weapons was a genius, Takeshi thought. *I wonder if we'll ever know who they were or why they left this place?*

Then the time for asking questions was over. Takeshi pressed his attack on the damaged Crawler, knocking the legs out from under it. The robot pilot ejected and made it to the second Crawler. Takeshi tore the prison pod off the wrecked robot machine and gently lifted the human prisoner out. The man was unconscious but seemed

unhurt. Takeshi recognized him as a fellow miner.

"Take it easy," he said, even though he knew the man couldn't hear him. "I'll get you back to Sentai Fortress. Your war is over for now, my friend."

Something struck the ground near the Blade Titan and began to spark. Takeshi looked up to see that an Iron Condor was coming in for an attack. As much as he wanted to fight, he knew he had to get the human prisoner to safety first. He fired a proton blast to drive the Iron Condor off and made for the safety of one of the buildings, with the human in the arms of his battle machine.

The Iron Condor did not pursue. Instead, it flew into the building that housed the computer and landed atop the giant machine. It attached a small component to the computer. In response, the computer repeated everything it had said to the EXO-

FORCE pilots, word for word. All of this was recorded and transmitted back to the robot base. Meca One would now know the first of the many secrets of the Golden City.

Once that was done, the Iron Condor flew off to seek out the coordinates the computer had given for the location of the next code.

光　光　光

While inside the Cyclone Defender, Ryo spotted the Shadow Crawler trying to make a getaway from the battle site. He knew his small battle machine wouldn't have the raw power it took to stop the robots, but he had to try.

He hoped to sneak up behind the robots, but the Cyclone Defender he was piloting had other ideas. It charged forward and slammed into the back of the Shadow Crawler, blasters firing. One of the Crawler's legs reared up and batted the Defender away.

"Hey! Hey! Hey!" Ryo shouted as his battle machine tumbled end over end. "Okay, okay, next time I'll read the manual first!"

光 光 光

Hikaru was making progress with the Sky Guardian. He hadn't figured out what its huge sword did yet, but the particle beam rifle worked just fine. He had been able to hold off the two Iron Condors, if not bring them down, and that was something, considering how powerful the robot machines seemed to be.

His eyes picked up a sensor blip on the control panel screen. The third Iron Condor was headed farther into the city, but away from the fight. Its destination was familiar— it was heading for the same spot the computer had said the next code would be!

"Takeshi!" Hikaru shouted into what he hoped was a communicator. "There's an Iron Condor going after the next code! Stop it!"

光　光　光

Moments after receiving Hikaru's broadcast, the Blade Titan had made it to the hiding place of the next code. The doors to the building had been torn off. The Iron Condor was already inside.

Takeshi thought fast. A full-scale battle would wreck the building and probably destroy the code, making the computer useless. What he needed was a way to win quickly, and the best way to do that was by losing. The key was the Iron Condor's rocket that could turn whatever it hit into a magnet. Add that to the fact that the code was on a metal plate, and he had the makings of a great plan.

He piloted the Blade Titan inside the building. The Iron Condor's pilot had already found the code, and it was in one of the battle machine's hands. "Hey, tinhead!" Takeshi broadcast over the Blade Titan's speakers.

"I hear they made you a pilot because you couldn't cut it as a toaster!"

The Iron Condor whirled and fired. Its weapon hit dead-on, immediately magnetizing the Blade Titan. The pull of the battle machine was as strong as Takeshi had hoped. The next instant, the metallic code plate had flown out of the Iron Condor's hand and affixed itself to Takeshi's battle machine.

"Want it? Come and get it," Takeshi said to the robot pilot. "Better hope your magnetic charge doesn't wear off too soon, though. Or didn't you see what my proton cannon can do yet?"

The robot pilot accessed the data. The battle had already been a fifty-seven percent success, since the location and other data on the city had been relayed back to base. It was important that the unit survive to report in person about the capabilities of the EXO-FORCE team's new battle machines. Logic dictated that it would be better to retreat and fight another day.

The Iron Condor rocketed up, smashing a hole through the roof. Sending out a coded signal, it beckoned the other two flying

robot battle machines to join it in retreat. Since one of the two was already damaged, thanks to Hikaru's sharpshooting, the robot pilots did what logic dictated: they fled.

Hikaru scanned the ground beneath him. The Blade Titan was intact but not moving. The Cyclone Defender was just getting to its feet. He decided it made more sense to regroup than risk being lured out of the city and ambushed, so he let the Iron Condors go.

光　　光　　光

Later, the three pilots stood in the computer chamber. They had exited their new battle machines, Ryo with great reluctance—Takeshi had to promise him he could take the Cyclone Defender back to Sentai Fortress for study. Now they were ready to enter the second code.

"What do you think it will tell us this time?" asked Takeshi.

"No idea," Hikaru replied. "I'm more worried about that Iron Condor. If the robots know about all this, especially the computer and the codes, they won't stop at anything to seize the city."

"Then we'll just have to stop them ourselves," said Ryo.

With a smile of anticipation, he punched the second code into the keypad. The computer whirred to life once more.